GLACIAL CHASE

Contents

by Keira Wong
illustrated by Douglas Fong

H   A   U   S

Reading Manga:
What is it?

The Japanese word 'manga' has been used for nearly 200 years. It means whimsical pictures (man = whimsical, ga = pictures).

Today, manga is a label for Japanese-style graphic novels, comic books and animated movies (also called anime). What's the difference between a graphic novel and a comic book? The answer is in your hands. Graphic novels are usually quality productions, sometimes run to hundreds of pages, and often cover serious subjects. Many Japanese manga focus on topics like the environment, the law, science, history – you name it.

Manga don't all look exactly the same, but they have some things in common:

Big Eyes

Oversized
Expressions

Fast Action

Reading Manga: How to Follow

Each page of a graphic novel is divided into boxes called panels. You follow the panels from left to right and top to bottom, like this:

Each panel is like a paragraph in a regular book. It shows you where the characters are, and what they are doing, saying and thinking.

Some panels include a little box at the top (or the bottom), giving you information about what's going on. These are called captions.

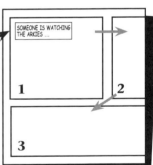

SOMEONE IS WATCHING THE ARKIES ...

DID YOU KNOW?

Traditional Japanese manga look a little different. That's because in Japan, people read from right to left. Japanese manga is read like this:

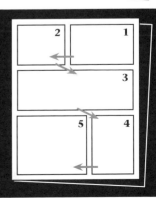

It's easier than it looks!

Reading Manga: Who's talking?

Speech balloons tell you who is speaking, what they're saying, and how.

Sometimes the lettering changes, to tell you which words are most important. These words might appear in **BOLD** or LARGE TYPE or in *ITALICS*.

Sometimes a punctuation point is enough to explain what's going on.

And how would you show an alien language? Maybe like this:

Reading Manga: What's that sound?

When you read speech bubbles, you hear manga characters' voices inside your head. There's a way to hear the background noises too – the rumble of thunder, the ringing of a telephone, the crack of a stick underfoot.

Manga artists represent sound effects (or SFX) by placing words over the panels, using lettering to suit each particular sound. It looks like this:

Scary sound   Mechanical sound   Quiet sound

DID YOU KNOW?

Japanese manga SFX are very precise. For example, *bicha bicha* means small splash, *bashan* is a medium splash, and *zaban* is a very big splash. There's even an SFX for total silence: *shiin*.

SFX are used to show emotions as well. The word *unzori* placed next to a character tells you they're feeling bored. If it was *moji moji* they'd be feeling shy, and *shobo shobo* indicates sadness.

Reading Manga:

What's that look on your face?

Manga characters have exaggerated expressions, to help you understand what they're feeling. The first feature everyone notices is the eyes, which may be wide open in:

Shock

Fear

Hope

Closed eyes can mean:

Laughter

Sadness

Noses and chins are more difficult to spot (some characters have no nose at all). This reflects the Japanese preference for delicate features. In manga, big noses and chins are kept for the bad guys.

Reading Manga:

What's that look on your face?

Just like manga characters' eyes, manga mouths are either huge or tiny. A big, wide-open mouth indicates:

Fear

Anger

Happiness

A character with a little mouth may be feeling:

Sad

Thoughtful

Shy

You can also tell a lot about manga characters from the crazy colour or style of their hair. For example, blue hair can mean the character is cool-headed, while orange hair equals determination (and sometimes a fiery temper). Wild, spiky hairstyles show the character is adventurous.

Characters

Earthlings

Molly

Molly is sporty and adventurous and friendly to everyone – even aliens from strange planets.

James

Molly's friend James is always ready for a new challenge. Just as well.

Halycrusians

Z-koo

A Halycrusian leader, who is honest, fair-minded and keen to explore his world with Molly and James.

K-la

Z-koo's niece. She doesn't always think before acting, and this can lead to trouble ...

B-roc

B-roc is a laid-back guy – always on the lookout for something to eat.

A SECOND SWINE HAS CRASHED INTO THE FIRST, AND THE CHASE IS ON AGAIN ...

JAMES SPOTS THE WAY OUT. IT LEADS TO A SHEER CLIFF FACE ...

THIS DOESN'T LOOK GOOD, GUYS!

GERAGHH!

WE HAVE TO STOP!

AND TAKE OUR CHANCES WITH THE SWINE?

JUST KEEP HOLD OF EACH OTHER!

WE *HAVE* TO STOP!!

GERAGHH!

A FEW HOURS LATER ...

HEY GUYS! IT'S K-LA AND B-ROC. ARE YOU OK?

DOES IT LOOK LIKE WE'RE OK?

LISTEN, I'M ONLY HERE BECAUSE Z-KOO CONTACTED US!

MAYBE WE DON'T WANT YOUR HELP, LIKE YOU DIDN'T WANT MINE WHEN WE WERE CAUGHT IN THE FLASH FLOOD!

GUYS, COOL IT! LET'S DEAL WITH ONE CRISIS AT A TIME!

IF YOU WANT ...

OK, TIME OUT! WE MADE A LADDER OUT OF BEJAIS. IT SHOULD BE LONG ENOUGH. JUST "HANG" IN THERE FOR A FEW MORE SECONDS.

GROAN ...

SO, HOW WAS IT?

WELL, THE SWINE ARE BIGGER THAN WE THOUGHT. MUCH BIGGER.

AND "CHASE THE SWINE" IS NOT THE BEST NAME FOR THE GAME. MORE LIKE THE OTHER WAY ROUND.

WHY? THEY DIDN'T LIKE TO BE CHASED?

NO, THEY DID THE CHASING AND WE DID THE RUNNING ... OR SLIDING.

SLIDING?

NEVER MIND. WE'LL TELL YOU THE WHOLE STORY ON THE WAY HOME.

GERAGHH!

THEY DON'T SOUND THAT BIG ...

THAT WAS GREAT! BUT NOBODY WOULD WANT TO MEET THOSE SWINE AGAIN!

AS LONG AS THEY STAY IN THE ICE MOUNTAINS AND Z-KOO DOESN'T TREK UP THERE, IT'LL NEVER HAPPEN!

SO – SAME TIME, SAME PLACE, NEXT WEEK?

YOU BET!

MOLLY AND JAMES WILL TRAVEL TO HALYCRUS AGAIN. AND ONE DAY, FAR IN THE FUTURE, OTHER KIDS MAY FIND THE PORTAL TO A VERY CHANGED HALYCRUS ...

Bejais Jewel-like baubles found in rocks. Can be made into almost anything. Also the Halycrusians' only food.

Halycrus An alternative world.

Halycrusians Inhabitants of Halycrus.

Mind message A thought, sent to another being to communicate.

Mind-reading The ability to hear another being's thoughts.

Mountain swine Massive blue hairy beast from Halycrus. Dangerous.

Portal A doorway into an alternative world.

Portal mixture An unusual blend of chemicals, which opens portals to other worlds.

Upper Ice Mountains Mountains towering high above the lowlands of Halycrus. They are riddled with ice caves.